Who can help Will Allen find the monster that lurks in the darkness?

None other than Bigelow Hawkins, the Great Monster Detective!

"Go sit in the middle of the room," the detective ordered.

I instantly obeyed. My parents would have died of shock if they knew.

"Good," he said. "Now, whatever you hear, just stay where you are."

"*Whatever you hear*? What does *that* mean?"

But Bigelow just said, "Hush now," so I sat there, alone in the middle of the room. I know it sounds crazy, but I could swear the walls were creeping closer...

ISBN 10 : 0-9789512-0-4
ISBN 13 : 978-0-9789512-0-7

Library of Congress Catalog # 2006936332

Illustrations copyright © 2007 by Jeffrey Friedman
Text copyright © 2004 by Jeffrey Friedman

First Printing - Halloween 2007
Printed in the U.S.A.

This book is rated **level II** in the **Rogue Bear Press** *AcceleReader* Program. It is designed for children 7-12 years of age.

Learn more about our *AcceleReader* Program at our website, **RogueBearPress.com.**

Teachers and Librarians take note :

Special sales discounts are offered to schools and libraries. Discounts are available for purchases of as little as 5 copies.

Check our website for details about our discount program.

Jason Edwards

Rogue Bear Press
New York

Books by Jason Edwards:

The Chronicles of the Monster Detective Agency:

Will Allen and the **Great Monster Detective**

Will Allen and the **Ring of Terror**

Will Allen and the **Hideous Shroud**

Will Allen and the **Terrible Truth**

Will Allen and the **Unconquerable Beast**

Will Allen and the **Dubious Shrine**

Will Allen and the **Lair of the Phantoms**

Will Allen and the **Greatest Mystery of All**

To Jenna and Jessica,

hoping that all your monsters
will be little ones

To Grace —
Be Brave!

Ron Edwards

Contents

Chapter One – The Problem Solvers

You know, I've never been a big fan of Sherlock Holmes. My dad calls him the world's greatest detective, but a stinky old pipe-smoker is just not my idea of a hero. My name is Will Allen. You'd never guess that I'm a detective myself, especially since I'm not one of those... well, *detective*-looking kinds of guys: you know, the ones who are big and tough with faces like stone. Well I'm nothing like that, in fact, I'm one of the shortest and scrawniest kids in my whole school. Still, a little person can solve some really big problems, and I've cracked some of the biggest, strangest cases you could ever imagine. But not one of them was any stranger than how I got started doing this in the first place.

I wasn't always a detective, you see. I mean sure, sometimes my mom would say something like, "That's amazing Will! How did you know I baked cookies while you were out? I aired out the kitchen so you wouldn't smell them!" and I would tell her, "Easy, mom. There's a trace of flour on the counter, the oven door is warm, and you hid something in the breadbox real fast when I came in."

And every now and then my dad would say something like, "Will, how did you ever find my golf club? I've been looking for it for days!" and I would answer, "Simple, dad. I knew that the last time you practiced in the yard, you trimmed the shrubs after, so I looked behind the rack where the pruning shears go."

Yeah, I've always been kind of a natural when it comes to solving mysteries.

Well, most mysteries, anyway. Sometimes even **I** needed help, which is where my story begins.

You see, I had this problem. But it wasn't a lost toy or anything.

I had a monster under my bed.

No, I mean *really*.

I know it sounds strange. You're probably thinking:

A monster? Oh, come on!

But it was real. Only no one would believe me.

Certainly not my parents.

"I have a monster under my bed," I said to my dad one morning as he sat at the table hiding behind his daily newspaper. He glared at me over the top of the Business Section.

"We don't believe in monsters," he replied, then ruffled the paper and turned to the next page. That didn't exactly make me feel better, so I went to my mom, who was in the kitchen putting our breakfast plates into the dishwasher.

"I have a monster under my bed," I told her.

"Well, don't invite it to tea," she answered without looking up. "We're down to four cups already, and some invisible monster always seems to break things around here."

I didn't think she was very funny.

I decided not to tell anyone at school about the monster, because most kids will give you a weird look or something if you tell them stuff like that. But I did tell my friend, Jeannine. She's almost as good at solving mysteries as I am, and we've always helped each other with problems and stuff, so I knew I could count on her.

"I have a monster under my bed," I whispered quietly as we sat together on the bus to school. She gave me a weird look. Go figure.

Of course, a weird look from Jeannine is a little different from other people's weird looks, mostly because Jeannine looks a little weird to begin with, seeing as how she likes to dye her hair all different colors and hang paperclips from her ears.

"Oh, Will," she said. "It's not fair! You always have the coolest things happen to you."

Now I gave *her* a weird look.

"What's so cool about a monster under my bed?" I asked.

"Well, it's way cooler than the plain old dust bunnies I have under mine," she answered.

Personally, I didn't think a monster under my bed was cool at all.

"At least dust bunnies don't try to lure you under the bed so they can eat you," I pointed out.

Jeannine thought about that for a minute.

"Well, okay, there's *that*," she finally said. "But still, it's *way* interesting."

"It is not!" I growled. "We're 5th graders now, Jeannine! 5th graders don't have monsters! It is definitely *not* cool!"

"It *could* be," Jeannine insisted. "It depends on what kind of monster it is. What does yours look like?"

"I don't know," I said. "I've never actually gotten a good look at it. It only comes out when it's really dark."

"You've never seen it?" Her face went sour, like it does when she sees that her mom has given her a bag of snow peas for snack again. "Then how do you even know you have a monster?"

"It makes noises," I told her. "Like…weird scratching and gurgling sounds."

"Maybe it's a chipmunk," she said.

My cheeks started to burn. Believe me, you don't want to be around when they get really fired up.

"Don't you think I thought of that?" I growled. "When I check during the day, nothing is there. No scratch marks. No nutshells. And I looked over every inch of the walls and ceiling. There are no holes or cracks that it could come in through."

"Maybe it's a mouse crawling under the floorboards."

"It's not coming from under the floorboards!" I hissed. "And mice don't grab your quilt and pull it under your bed while you sleep so that you'll get cold and come down after it. Only monsters do that!"

Jeannine just gave me a blank stare.

"So, I guess you have a monster under your bed," she finally said.

"Exactly," I agreed.

"So, what are you going to do about it?" She replied without missing a beat.

"I'm not sure," I said. "I tried to set a trap for it, but I couldn't lure it out into the open."

"What did you use as bait?" she asked.

"A brownie ice cream sundae," I told her. "I figured that would attract almost anything."

Jeannine looked quite shocked.

"And it *didn't work*?" she gasped.

"Nope," I replied. "Plus my parents yelled at me when the ice cream melted all over the floor."

Jeannine scratched her head, which is what she does when she tries to think too hard. Only this time, she came up with a really good idea.

"What we need," she said, "is an expert."

I gaped at her with a *why didn't I think of that* look on my face.

"That's a very good idea," I said. Jeannine smiled.

"Thank you," she said.

"Where do you suppose we could find someone like that?" I asked.

Jeannine stopped smiling. She started scratching her head again. Just then, the bus pulled into the school parking lot.

"Well, I'm sure we'll think of something by this afternoon," she said. And then without another word, she got up and walked off the bus. Some people get annoyed when she does stuff like that, but to me that's just Jeannine being Jeannine. A few seconds later, I followed.

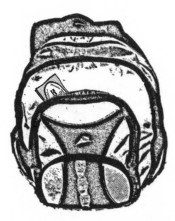

Chapter Two – Secondary Troubles

In the two months since we had started there, Jeannine and I decided that Ashford Middle School was a pretty decent place, but I had a rather bad day there that day, owing to my getting caught by Mrs. McAllister leafing through the yellow pages when I was supposed to be doing math problems.

"And what do you think you are doing?" she said as she walked over and stood above me.

"Um, I'd rather not say," I told her.

For some reason, Mrs. McAllister got very stern. Her painted-on black eyebrows, which clashed sharply with her silver-grey hair, rose high above her thick, horn-rimmed glasses.

"You will explain yourself this instant, or go to the principal's office!" she roared.

I just looked down.

"Well?" she said impatiently.

"I'm thinking it over," I said.

Mrs. McAllister's pale cheeks turned red. She grabbed the book.

"The yellow pages?" Her face changed from angry to puzzled. "Why are you looking for...an exterminator?"

"I...ah, have a pest problem at home."

"I see," she growled. "And you are looking for an exterminator...in *my* math class? Why aren't your parents taking care of this?"

"They don't take math," I said.

I got a lot of extra homework to do that day.

When I got on the bus to go home, Jeannine had already saved me a seat, just as she has ever since second grade.

"So, I figured out where to find an expert!" she said happily.

"Really?" I said gratefully. "Where?"

"Just check the yellow pages!" she answered. "Look under 'E' for *exterminators.*"

I gave her a nasty look.

"What?" she said. "What did I say?"

"Never mind," I told her. "I already looked."

"You didn't find any ads for exterminators?"

"Not the kind I need."

"Then what's *that*?" she said, pointing at my book bag.

"What's what?" I asked.

"That card sticking out of your bag," she answered. She tilted her head slantways, and read, "M-O-N-S-T-..." Her head popped upright again. "That's all I can see, but I'm pretty sure it says monster."

I just looked at my bag. Sure enough, there was a card sticking out. I pulled it out of my bag and read it out loud.

"Look," I said. "There's a handwritten note on the back of the card."

"What does it say?" Jeannine asked.

"It says, '*If you need me, hang a red flag out your window.*'"

I just stared at the card.

"Well, it looks like you found your expert monster hunter," Jeannine said.

I shook my head. "I didn't. It looks like *he* found *me*."

"Whatever," she said with a wave of her hand. "The point is: your problem is solved."

I wasn't so sure.

"But how did he find me? How did he know I was looking for a...I mean, I didn't tell anyone but you about my..."

I looked all around the bus to be sure no one was listening.

"...My you know what."

"Maybe someone heard us this morning," Jeannine answered.

"So then you think someone on the bus knows where to find a monster detective, and put the card in my bag?" I said skeptically. "I doubt it. It's probably just a prank."

Jeannine rolled her eyes.

"Well, so what if it is? All it's asking you to do is

hang a flag out your window. Just do it and see what happens."

"But I don't have a red flag."

"A red shirt then," Jeannine insisted. "What's the difference?"

"Nope. I don't have one of those either."

Jeannine frowned, and started scratching her head again.

"Do you have a red flag I could borrow?" I asked her.

"No," she said. "My parents think red flags are un-American."

"A red shirt?"

"No. My mother says red is not my color."

"Do you have *anything* red?"

"Well, if you're desperate, I have some old red panties in the back of my drawer. I wouldn't mind you hanging *them* out a window."

I just looked at her.

"I'd rather be eaten by the monster," I said.

Jeannine got a little snippy after that.

"Suit yourself," she said, tilting her nose up and turning away.

Girls can be so moody sometimes. I tried to talk to her some more after that, but she just told me that I'd have to figure something out on my own.

When I got home, I went to my room and started my homework, but I didn't get much done. I sat at my desk beneath my Chicago Cubs pennant and poster of Albert Einstein, the only things hanging on the annoyingly cheerful blue wallpaper, and was busy coloring in the 'O's on my second sheet of math problems when an idea hit me. I hunted down my dad's Fourth of July American Flag and rolled it up halfway, so that only the red and white stripes showed. Then I started coloring in the white stripes with red magic marker. That's when my mom came in. Her dirty blonde curls were wrapped in a hairnet and her smock was covered in fresh splatters of paint, so I knew she'd just come from her studio in the basement.

"Are you doing homework?" she asked.

"Um, sort of..." I answered.

Oops. Never say *'sort of'* to a mom. It makes her think you're up to something.

My mom came over for a closer look, and when she saw
what I was doing, her eyes popped out.

No, I don't mean *out of her head and rolling on the
floor* out, she just got all bug-eyed.

"Will!" she cried out in horror. "What have you
done?"

I looked up at her.

"Is that a trick question?" I asked.

"The flag!" she shouted. "Our American flag! You've ruined it!"

I looked back down at the flag. Three stripes were colored in, and one was halfway finished.

"They're washable markers, mom."

"Give me that this instant!"

"But mom, I need it..."

"This instant!" she shouted. Her cheeks were as red as the flag, so I knew there was no point in arguing. I handed her the flag.

"I'm going to speak to your father about this!" she said in that *'I'm going to speak to your father'* kind of voice that she has. "Messing up the flag! Do you know you could go to jail for that?"

"Do the beds there have monsters under them?" I asked.

My mom just stormed out. Personally, I don't see what the big deal was all about, but there's something about flags that makes grownups act weird. But now, I was back to square one, with no flag, and no monster hunter.

"I'd better put on my thinking cap," I said to myself.

No, I am *not* too old for a thinking cap.

Anyway, I don't actually have a cap, but just saying that somehow makes me think better. And sure enough, I came up with another idea. But I figured I'd better wait until after dinner to test out my new plan so that my mom wouldn't catch me again. So, after sitting down at the table that evening to a meal with a French name that my mom took twenty minutes trying to get me to pronounce, but which *I* called, "old socks with brown sauce," I went back up to my room and got out a white t-shirt from my underwear drawer. I tied the sleeves together around the end of my baseball bat, and when I hung it sideways, it sort of looked like a flag.

"Now I just have to make it red," I told myself. But I had already used up all the ink in my red makers, so I went to the kitchen and got some fruit punch from the refrigerator. I took the bottle back to my room and poured the drink all over the white shirt. When it was pretty much soaked, I stopped and held it up. It was kind of blotchy and purplish, but hey, I figured maybe it's close enough. I took my bat and jammed it into my clothes hamper, and then moved it to the window and hung the shirt through the opening. Then I closed the window as much as I could and hoped for the best. All of a sudden, a creepy voice came from right behind me.

Chapter Three – A Most Unusual Detective

"I knew you'd call," spoke a squeaky, yet gravelly kind of voice. I turned around really fast, and there, standing next to my bed, was a very, very small person in a very, very big trench coat and bowler hat. Aside from a shiny gold badge on the ratty old coat, I couldn't see much: the coat covered everything right down to the ground, including his hands and feet, and a dark, fuzzy nose and a mess of scraggly brown hair were all that poked out from under the brim of the hat.

"Are you the monster hunter?" I asked.

"Detective," the gravelly voice replied, pointing proudly at his badge. "Monster *Detective*. Bigelow J. Hawkins at your service."

He looked more like a munchkin in disguise.

"Aren't you a little short for a detective?"

"Size isn't everything," Bigelow answered. "A little person can solve some really big cases. I myself have uncovered some of the biggest monsters there are."

"And you can get rid of them?"

Bigelow gave me a strange look. At least I think he did, because his face barely showed from under his hat, but he slouched as though he was sad.

"I usually don't have to. Once we find your monster, all we have to do is shine some light on it. Monsters hate light."

"That makes them disappear?"

He gave me that look again.

"No. That makes them...less scary. And monsters that aren't scary don't have much reason to hang around."

"Oh," I said. "Well, that sounds good enough for me. Let's get started."

"We can't. Not yet," Bigelow said.

"What? Why not?"

"It's not dark yet. I told you, monsters don't like the light. They won't come out until nighttime. That's when we'll uncover them."

He then walked over to the light switch on my wall and

turned it off. The room darkened somewhat, but light continued to filter in from my window, making my room glow eerily.

"Um, what should we do until then?" I asked.

"Well, for a start, let's discuss my fee," Bigelow answered. My face went sour.

"Your fee?" I said rather crossly. "Your card said there wasn't any fee."

"You must have read it wrong," Bigelow insisted. "Look again. It says 'No fee *unless successful*'."

I took out the card, which I'd kept in my pocket since the bus ride from school, and read it over.

"Huh. How about that?" I said. "Well, how much do you..."

"Oh, I don't accept cash," Bigelow said. "But I believe you have an old teddy bear that you don't play with anymore. I'd like that."

I looked at him, and tried to lean so that I could see under the brim of his hat, but it was too dark to see his face.

"You want to be paid with a toy?" I said. "Are you serious?"

"That's my price," he answered firmly, "for helping you solve your monster problem. Do you want my help or not?"

Like it or not, I needed help. I went to my toy chest and dug down to the bottom until I uncovered Teddy. He was a little ratty, but still soft and warm.

"But...I don't want to give him up." I pouted.

"You don't play with him anymore."

"I know. But I still want him."

"I promise," he said in a voice that sounded much less gravelly, "that I will take good care of him, and give him a home where he'll always be happy."

I looked down at Teddy. I swear it almost looked like he smiled.

"Okay," I said, and handed him to Bigelow. At that very moment, the room turned dark. The cheerful blue color fled from my walls, turning them to shades of mud.

"What...what's happening?" I asked, looking around nervously.

"They're coming," Bigelow whispered. "Night is falling."

"But how did it get dark so fast?"

"Never mind," he grumbled. "Let's just get ready. Where's your Revealer?"

"My what?"

"Your Revealer," Bigelow said. "You know, a flashlight that can shine some light on the monsters."

"I...I don't have one," I whispered nervously. Right then, it got *much* darker. The air around us grew thick with an inky mist, and the shadows from the trickle of light that dripped in through the window crawled all around us. But Bigelow ignored all that.

"Here, have this one," Bigelow whispered back, handing me a plain-looking red flashlight from behind his back. I turned it on to be sure it worked.

"Don't turn it on yet!" he hissed. "You'll scare him off!" I turned the flashlight off quickly.

"Sorry," I said quietly. "What do we do now?"

"We wait," he answered.

So we sat there in the dark, as quiet as mice for the better part of an hour. Finally, Bigelow got up, turned on his flashlight, and paced around the room.

"This isn't working," he muttered.

"Does that mean I get Teddy back?"

Bigelow turned to face me. There in the dark, he seemed much bigger than he had earlier.

"What we need," he grumbled, "is to set a trap."

"I already tried that," I told him.

"What did you use as bait?"

"A brownie ice-cream sundae."

Bigelow seemed shocked.

"And it *didn't work*?" he gasped.

"No," I said.

Bigelow scratched his head, doing the same thinking scratch that Jeannine did all the time.

"I have an idea," he announced.

"Really? What?"

"We need different bait," he said. "I think I know what will lure him out into the open."

"What do we need?"

Bigelow just looked at me. As he turned his head up, I

thought for a second that I saw his eyes glow from under that bowler hat.

"Go sit in the middle of the room," he ordered. I instantly obeyed. My parents would have died of shock if they knew.

"Good," he said. "Now, whatever you hear, just stay where you are."

"*Whatever you hear*? What does *that* mean?"

But Bigelow just said, "Hush now," so I sat there, alone in the middle of the room. I know it sounds crazy, but I could swear the walls were creeping closer, and as the shadows grew deeper, I shuddered from a sudden chill.

"N…Now what?" I stuttered.

"Now just listen," he whispered.

I listened, but the darkness seemed to be sucking all the sound right out of the air. Just when it seemed as if nothing could break through, I heard a swooshing and rustling sound.

"Is that it?" I asked. "Is that the monster?"

Bigelow then did a strange thing. Even though it was

very dark, he pulled out a magnifying glass, put it to his eye, and scanned the room.

"No," he finally answered. "That's just the wind blowing through the trees."

I listened harder. Deep in the mist, there was a creepy, creaking sound.

"That's it, isn't it?" I whispered fiercely. Bigelow scanned again.

"No," he said. "Just loose floorboards."

The whooshing and creaking died away, and it grew very quiet. There in the stillness, the shadows became like living things, closing in on me like hungry wolves. That's when I heard something else, something that made goose-bumps pop up on my skin.

It was a scratching sound coming from under the bed. Then there was a gurgling, and I looked all around to see what it was. But all I saw was darkness.

"B...Bigelow? Is that you?"

But Bigelow didn't answer. All I heard was the gurgling sound, which grew into a growl, like that of an empty stomach. It seemed to be moving all around me.

And it was getting closer.

Chapter Four – Nightfall

The situation was bad. I sensed that I was in terrible danger.

Danger of dumping a load into my undershorts, that is. One more second and I would have needed some toilet tissue, a mop, and a new pair of pants, but just then my door opened and light poured into the room. My father walked in and said, "Will! Why are you sitting in the dark? Don't you know it's bad for your eyes?" And he turned on the light.

"There, that's better. What were you doing in here?"

I just looked around. Bigelow was nowhere to be seen, but my teddy bear now sat on my bed next to the pillow. I went to look under the bed when my father stopped me.

"Are you hiding something under there?"

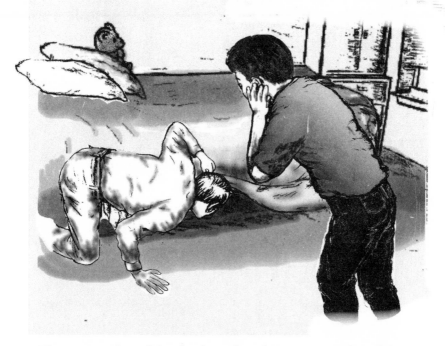

He stooped and looked under, but I guess he didn't see anything, because he stood right back up and looked around. That's when he noticed Teddy.

"What's *that* doing here?" He reached to pick him up, but I rushed and grabbed him first. When I squeezed him close, away from my father's grasp, I swear I felt him grow warm all over.

"Oh, for Pete's sake," my dad said irritably. "Aren't you getting a little old for a teddy bear?"

I didn't say anything. I just clung on to Teddy. I don't know if it was Teddy or me, but one of us wanted to scratch his eyes out.

I don't think it was Teddy.

"What do you want, dad?" I grumbled in a surly tone. "Are you looking to borrow another comic book?"

My dad blushed. Now, I knew my mother must have sent him to scold me about the flag, but I could tell by the way he was scrunching his eyebrows that he had forgotten why he had come, and I certainly wasn't going to help him remember.

"Never mind," my father finally said. "Just get ready for bed. And get rid of that…that horrible *thing*."

I froze. Had he spotted Bigelow? Or the Monster?

"What thing?" I said, looking all around. "Where?"

"I meant the bear," he said, and left, closing the door behind him. Right away, I began searching the room for Bigelow. As I rifled through my closet to see if he was hiding there, I heard it again: the scratching noise under my bed. I slowly walked on over, then bent down and thrust the flashlight ahead of me as I looked underneath.

There was Bigelow, his magnifying glass held close to his eye, bent over inspecting the floorboards.

"Bigelow!" I shouted. "There you are!"

Bigelow looked up at me, and through the magnifying glass his eye looked like a huge, hairy crystal ball.

"Well of course I'm *here*," he said irritably. "Where else would you look for a monster that's under your bed?"

"But...But there's nothing there," I said. "My dad just looked."

It was hard to tell, but I could swear he rolled his eyes at me.

"Grownups," he grumbled. "Don't know monsters from meatballs."

I thought for a second.

"That explains last night's dinner," I said.

"Never trust a grownup to find a monster," Bigelow insisted. "I've never yet met one who can."

"What are you saying?" I asked. "That grownups can't see monsters?"

"Just the opposite," he answered gruffly. "They see them *everywhere*. But their monsters look a lot different than yours. They look like a neighbor who might be a kidnapper, or the new manager who might steal their job, or the new building that's going to cut off their scenic views and lower their property values. And so they just can't imagine how monsters could look anything like what yours do."

I thought about all that for a minute.

"What…what do *my* monsters look like?" I asked.

Bigelow pursed his lips.

"We'll see," he said, and then he walked over to the light switch and turned it off once more. It went nearly pitch black, and I trembled as the shadows sprang back to life. My head twitched back and forth, scanning the room for any sign of movement, when suddenly the scratching sound came back. It echoed off every wall, and I turned on my flashlight and pointed it all around the room.

"Not yet!" Bigelow shouted. "Turn it off!"

"But…how can I find the monster if I can't see him?"

"Don't worry," Bigelow assured. "He'll find *you*."

I didn't like the sound of that at all.

"But I don't want him to find me!" I cried. "I just want him to go away!"

"Will," he said in as calm and steady a tone as his squeaky, gravelly voice could manage, "this is the only way. If you don't turn off the light, you'll never be rid of the monster. Never."

My shaking hands turned and shined the flashlight right at him, the very flashlight he had put in my grasp. Bigelow squinted, but didn't flinch.

"Be brave, Will," he said. "You can do it."

Someone more sensible than me would probably have thought twice before turning off the light in a room with a lurking monster, which to me seemed kind of like lighting a match in a dynamite factory, but for some reason, I trusted Bigelow. I turned off my flashlight.

"Good," he said, as the scratching noise grew into a growl again. "What do you hear?"

"A monster." I answered. "And he sounds hungry."

"Is he...saying anything?"

"What would he say?" I asked tersely. "Lunchtime?"

Even over the growling, I could hear Bigelow scratch his head.

"All right," he grumbled. "Let's try something. Act like you're really scared."

"Try to act scared?" I snarled. "What a *great* idea. I'd rather try staying off tonight's menu! I'm turning on the light."

I flicked the switch on my flashlight, but nothing happened. My knees started shaking.

"Uh, Bigelow…the flashlight…"

My breath became frosty, and the growling grew much louder, so loud that it became a roar.

"That's it, that's it," Bigelow urged. "Now, what do you hear?"

"A…a roaring," I said through chattering teeth. "Wait, it sounds like…"

Rising above the roaring was another gurgling, and then a sloshing sound.

"It sounds like…"

A glub-glubbing sound replaced the sloshing. That's when it hit me.

"It sounds like…*a toilet flushing*!"

"Now!" Bigelow shouted. "Turn on your Revealer and shine the light on it now!"

"But mine doesn't work!"

"Oh, nonsense!" Bigelow insisted. "Try again!"

I flicked the switch, and the beam came right on.

Then I kind of wished it was still broken.

Chapter Five – What Lurks in the Darkness

I swung the beam of light up and down and it showed, bit by bit, the form of what stood before me. At first there was just a shiny gleam from the smooth white surface. Then I saw a reflection from a bright brass handle and foaming water splashing out the sides.

"It…it can't be…" I mumbled.

But as impossible as it might seem, there in the middle of my room was a giant *toilet*, stretching from the floor almost to the ceiling, with big bulging eyes on top and rows of sharp, shark-like teeth sticking out from between the seat and the bowl.

"B…Bigelow?" I called out weakly.

"I'm here, Will," he answered.

"Bigelow?" I repeated. "I…I have to pee!"

35

"Not now!" he shouted. "Fight it!"

"I *am* fighting it!" I protested. "But I really have to go!"

"I meant the *monster*," Bigelow growled. "Fight it! Use the light!"

I couldn't believe what I was hearing.

"You want me to fight a ten foot tall man-eating toilet…with a flashlight?"

"With your *bravery*!" he urged. "You can do it, Will! I know you have it in you!"

Personally, I was thinking less about having *it* in *me*, and more about that toilet having *me* in *it*.

"No way!" I shouted, as I backed away from the monster. As I did, it grew even bigger, until it seemed that the walls would split open.

This would have been a very good time for my dad to remember to come in and scold me for the whole flag incident, don't you think?

Well, that didn't happen, though how the noise and the rumbling and the shaking floors could go unnoticed by two people who caught me bowling in my room because the falling pins woke them up I'll never know. The point is, no one came, so it was just me, Bigelow, and the monster toilet.

"Don't worry! I know just what to do!" Bigelow shouted, and ran past me and stood right in front of the monster. The monster leaned back and roared, then its jaws came flying forward and with one great snap, Bigelow was gone.

"Oh m-m-my…" I stuttered. "It…It *ate* him!"

A big grin spread across the toilet as it licked its lips and then turned back to me, eying me hungrily.

I stumbled back as those dripping teeth came at me. The monster growled, and then lunged forward again, snapping at my legs. I dove back, but the monster drew closer, until I was backed up against the wall. With no retreat left, I gazed into the sneering eyes of the monster as its gleaming teeth rose above my head...

Just then, Bigelow sprung out from behind the monster! He hadn't been eaten, but had run past the crashing jaws to my bed, and now he was running back to me, carrying something in his hands.

"Here!" he shouted. "You need this!"

As he shoved it into my arms, I looked down to see what he had brought.

It was Teddy.

"What's this for?" I shouted, utterly bewildered. "Is he going to grow into a real bear and fight this thing?"

"Hold him!" Bigelow instructed. "Hug him!"

"Hug him? I'm fighting for my life with a flashlight and a hug?"

But when you're desperate, you'll try anything, so I gave Teddy a squeeze. He felt so warm! I don't know how, but it soothed me a bit, in spite of the dreadful monster in front of me.

"That's it!" Bigelow shouted. "Now, use the light!"

As I clung to Teddy, I turned back to face the monster. It glared at me with those hungry eyes and then reared back and roared ferociously. Somehow, though its roar struck me like a brick, the monster seemed a bit smaller than a moment ago. I pointed my flashlight right at it. The monster squinted, and squirmed, and then finally screamed as though it had been caught in flame rather than light. And then, amazingly, it began to *shrink*.

"That's it!" Bigelow shouted. "Don't stop now! You're doing it!"

I held the light steady, and the toilet kept getting smaller and smaller. When it was down to five feet tall, it began to cower, and retreated back toward the bed.

"Don't let it go back under!" Bigelow instructed. "Keep the light between the bed and the monster!"

I did as he told me, and backed the monster up into the corner of the room.

"Well done!" Bigelow exclaimed. "There's no escape now!"

The toilet kept getting smaller, until it was only a few inches high. Then, the shrinking stopped. It looked like a freaky happy meal toy.

"What happened?" I asked. "Why did it stop shrinking?"

"That's about as small as that one gets," Bigelow

said.

"What? But then how do I get rid of it?"

"You don't," Bigelow explained. "It will be with you as long as it wants to be."

"What? You mean this monster could be with me *forever*?"

Then I heard a noise, a gurgling, sloshing sound. I looked back at the monster.

It had grown. It was already the size of a real, full-grown toilet. And what was worse, I still had to pee.

"What help are you?" I shouted at Bigelow. "Look at that! What's to stop it from growing big again and eating me alive while I'm sleeping?"

"Use the light," Bigelow said calmly. "What do you see?"

I clung to Teddy and shined the light on the toilet.

"I see a monster," I said.

"Look again," he said. "Look harder."

I held the flashlight tightly, and moved closer.

"I see…" I said, "I see…"

In the glow of my flashlight, the eyes and teeth of the monster seemed to melt away.

"…I see a bowl made of clay, with a plastic seat on

top and water running through it."

"That doesn't sound very frightening," Bigelow said. "Go on. Look *deeper*."

"I see…" I tilted my head and squinted. "…I see an *image* inside. It looks like a little boy sitting on a toilet, crying for his mommy."

"Excellent!" Bigelow said. "What else?"

But right then, I just stopped.

"I don't need to look any more," I said, straightening back up. "I see it now. I finally see it clearly."

I turned off the light, but the gurgling sound was gone.

"It was *me*," I realized. "When I was three, I had to go to the bathroom in a department store, but the toilet was broken. It kept flushing while I was sitting on it. It was so loud! And I was afraid. Afraid that…"

"…That you would be sucked down the drain." Bigelow said.

"Yes."

"Turn the Revealer back on," Bigelow instructed. "What does the light show you now?"

I turned on the light. Even in the dark, the monster had shrunk back to toy size. I studied it closely.

"What do you see?" Bigelow asked. "Anything that

can hurt you?"

"No. I just see clay," I said. "Clay, and plastic, and water."

As I spoke, the monster grew smaller still. When it stopped shrinking this time, it was no bigger than a thimble. I picked it up in my hand. It snapped at me and tried to bite me, but its teeth were soft, and I didn't even feel it. It was like a dog trying to bite the wheel off a tank. I lifted my hand, with the monster still clinging to my finger with its gummy mouth, and swayed it back and forth.

"What do I do with it?" I asked.

"Put it on the shelf," Bigelow told me. "Just look at it once in a while, and it will never grow big again."

I walked over to my bookshelf, slid over a stack of mini-mysteries to make room, and squeezed the monster between the stack and a great big hardcover copy of the Baseball Records Book. The toilet's eyes scanned the huge towers of books surrounding it and cringed.

"So, that's it?" I asked, wiping my hands together happily. Bigelow gave me a grim look.

"No, I'm afraid not," he said. I looked at him sourly.

"What? Why not? Did we take care of this monster or not?"

Bigelow scratched his head, doing that Jeannine-type scratch that he did.

"I think," he whispered, "there are more of them."

Chapter Six – The Truth Comes Out

"More?" I said nervously. Behind me, the toilet monster whimpered. "What…What makes you think so?"

"Well, for one thing, I saw several different monster trails when I looked under your bed."

I thought about that.

"But how can you tell that means more than one monster? It could just be the same one making tracks on different nights."

Bigelow seemed offended.

"I am a Gold Shield Master Detective," he said huffily, pointing to the proud badge on his beat-up old coat. "And an *expert* monster detective such as myself can tell the difference between the tracks of different monsters."

"How?"

"All monsters are different," he explained. "But they can be categorized. The two main categories are simple: smart monsters and dumb monsters. That toilet was a dumb monster. He growled and roared and flashed his teeth to scare you. He couldn't even talk."

"And smart monsters?"

"A smart monster wouldn't give himself away so easily. They're much better at hiding, usually behind some other monsters like this one."

"So," I reasoned, "You think that this monster was just a decoy?"

Bigelow nodded.

"Or a pawn. You've been afraid of broken toilets since you were three. How long have you had a monster under your bed?"

I shrugged.

"A few weeks, I guess."

"Then a few weeks ago, something must have happened. Something that…well, that created a monster that can open a doorway to your room. And he's shoving any other monster he can find through the door at you, so that he stays safely hidden, free to attack again and again."

Though I was terrified by what he told me, I couldn't help being very impressed.

"That's brilliant, Bigelow," I said. "You really are a great monster detective."

He just shrugged modestly.

"I just know how they think," he said.

"Of course you do," I agreed. "After all, you're one of them, aren't you?"

Bigelow froze.

"What...What makes you say that?" he stuttered.

"Oh come on, Bigelow," I insisted. "You just appear in my room from out of nowhere. You grow when I'm scared just like the toilet-monster did. My dad couldn't see you under the bed. Either you're not very smart, which you've already proven isn't true, or you've been purposely dropping clues all over the place. You *wanted* me to figure it out."

Bigelow smiled a sharp toothy smile.

"You're a pretty good detective yourself," he said.

"Thanks. But what I don't understand," I went on, "is *why*."

"All monsters are different," he said again. "Those other monsters and I are different. We want different things."

I looked down into my arms.

"Teddy," I whispered, squeezing him tightly. "You want Teddy. But why?"

Bigelow stared at me

"How does it feel?" he asked longingly. "How do *you* feel when you hold him?"

"I feel...warm," I answered. "It feels like something is glowing inside me."

"*That's* it," Bigelow said. "I want to feel like that. That's what I want."

"Then, what is it the others want?" I asked.

Bigelow reached behind his back and pulled out an even bigger flashlight.

"That's what we have to find out," he said, and then he walked on over and flicked the switch, plunging the room back into darkness.

"Bigelow," I called out into the darkness. "How will I know when I've found him? The monster behind it all, I mean."

"You'll know," Bigelow assured me. "You already know what he looks like."

"I do?"

I wondered what Bigelow meant by that, but before he could explain, the scratching sound reappeared. It didn't seem nearly as scary as the first time I'd heard it, but then it grew much louder and busier than before, as if a whole kennel of dogs was trying to dig its way in through the ceiling, walls, and floor. It echoed louder and louder until it was a thunderous roar. Bigelow grabbed my arm, his furry fingers shaking uncontrollably.

"What's happening?" I asked.

"Uh, oh," Bigelow said weakly. "This is bad."

I turned to him.

"This is bad? *This is bad?* That is *not* what I want to hear right now, Bigelow!"

"He knows!" Bigelow screeched. "He knows we're on to him, so he's sending them all at us at once! Quick, turn on the light!"

I flicked the switch on my flashlight, but nothing happened.

"Oh, no!" I shouted. "It's broken again! What do I do now, Bigelow?"

He didn't answer. I grabbed his shaking hand and pulled him toward me.

"Bigelow!" I shouted, but he was frozen in place.

I could hear the scratching turn to a din of noises. There were roars, and screams, and crashes, and voices. And they were getting closer.

"Bigelow!" I pleaded. "Please, snap out of it!"

But he didn't move, or speak. He even stopped shaking. His arm was ice cold to my touch.

He...he's really frozen! He's actually scared stiff! I thought. And as the sounds of the monsters drew closer, I felt the cold grip of fear take hold of me as well.

But even as the cold tried to fill me, I felt a surge of warmth flow into me from the arm that held tightly to my Teddy. I looked down at my Bear, and then at Bigelow.

That's it! I realized. *I know what to do!*

"I know what you need, Bigelow!" I called out over the din. "Here, take this!"

And as the monsters drew near, I pressed Teddy into his hand. I thought that would revive him, but he remained frozen, and then the icy cold flooded *my* body as well.

Chapter Seven – The Hardest Part

For a moment, nothing happened, and I was sure I was about to end up as Monster Chow, but then the paw-like hand that held Teddy seemed to glow. Bigelow started to warm up, and then swayed, stumbled a bit, and shook his head.

"W...What..." he mumbled. "What happened..."

"Never mind that!" I said. "They're here, Bigelow! They're *here!*"

Bigelow straightened and looked all around the pitch-black room. He threw his shoulders back, handed Teddy back to me, and forcefully flicked on his flashlight. He put his furry hand on my flashlight, and it lit too.

"Nice trick," I grumbled.

Bigelow ignored me. Instead, he pointed the light into the air around us. Scads of strange creatures flew in every direction, scattering as the light struck.

"We have to work together," Bigelow commanded. "I'll take this side…" he pointed to his right. "…And you take those over there."

I turned to look where he had directed me, but all I saw was blackness. I crept slowly forward into what seemed like a sea of ink, when suddenly, out of the darkened corner Bigelow had pointed at, a flash of giant, razor-sharp teeth snapped right at my head, missing my face by inches.

"Yeeee!" I screeched. "Bigelow, what was that?"

But Bigelow didn't answer. Whatever it was shot through the air past me, and as it turned to make another pass, I caught sight of my attacker in the faint moonlight that fluttered in through my window, and the air caught in my throat as though I had forgotten how to breathe.

"Sh-Sh-*Shark*!" I gasped.

For there, to my horror, was a giant bloodthirsty shark swimming *right through the air*. It came flying at me again with its red-stained jaws swiping in every direction.

"Bigelow!" I cried. "Bigelow, help!"

But in an instant, it was already upon me. I dodged just in time, and when the monster spun around for another try, I swung my flashlight around and caught it full in the

face with the beam. The monster shark howled, thrashing about like a harpooned whale, and then fell crashing to the floor. I kept the light on it as it lay there, shrinking it until it turned into a guppy that flopped around like...well, like a fish out of water.

"I did it!" I shouted. "Bigelow, I did it!"

"Good work!" Bigelow called out. "Now, put it on the shelf with the other one."

But before I could pick it up, a deep, heavy rumbling growled menacingly, echoing from every direction.

"What...what was that?" I wondered as I glanced nervously about.

Just then, a crash of thunder shook the room like an earthquake, almost knocking me off my feet. I pointed my flashlight all around scanning for the source, but before I could spot anything, a blinding flash of lightning struck right at my feet, knocking me down.

"Yow! That was close!" I yelled. I tried to get up, but just as I lifted my head, another flash, like the beam from a ray-gun, erupted from above and whizzed past my face. I ducked, but from my knees I quickly pointed my flashlight up where the bolt had come from, and caught a monstrous storm in its beam. Its swirling blackness, even darker than the night, hung overhead, with smoky fingers billowing across the ceiling.

"Gotcha!" I cheered.

A raging thunder shook the room, but the dark cloud, unable to escape the beam of my flashlight, slowly began to fade. The rumbling softened, until it was replaced by the splashing of a gentle spring rain. I actually smiled at that, until I saw that the rain that had fallen was being sucked up by huge, twisted roots that were covering the floor. My eyes followed the trail of roots to a hideously deformed monster tree, which grew so fast that in seconds it had spread across half the room. Before I could move, its branches reached out and wound themselves around me, pulling me toward a horrible, gaping maw in the trunk.

"NO!" I screamed. "LET ME GO!"

But with my hands bound by the rope-like vines, my flashlight was stuck pointing uselessly at the ceiling as I was drawn bit-by-bit into that horrible, slimy mouth. Its evil eyes glowered at me as my feet sank deep into that moss-covered maw, while I struggled and squirmed with all my might.

"Bigelow!" I shouted. "Bigelow, where are you?"

There were grunting and growling sounds coming from where Bigelow had stood, but I could not turn my head to see what was happening, so I fought on alone, twisting and pulling at the branches. But I just sank in deeper.

"SURRENDERRRR," hissed the monster tree.
"GIVE IN TO YOUR FEARRR..."

"No Will!" I heard Bigelow shout. "Don't give up!

The hardest part of any battle is to keep on trying when things look hopeless. But you can beat this thing if you just don't quit!"

I took heart from Bigelow's voice, but I still kept sinking. I was in almost up to my thighs when I heard a cracking sound: my twisting and tugging had finally split one of the vines that bound me.

"Yes!" I cried. "I did it!"

Before another vine could grab my arm, I tore my hand loose and pointed the light point-blank at the face of the tree. It groaned a weepy moaning sound, and my legs slid out of its mouth to the floor as the monster spat and retched violently.

"You think I taste bad?" I quipped. "You should try my mother's casserole."

I kept the beam focused dead center on the trunk, which caused the tree to begin sprouting flowers all over its bare branches. Apparently, the monster tree found this very embarrassing, for it covered itself bashfully as it shrank, and then hopped away, owing to the lack of any legs, trying to escape. I was about to chase after it when Bigelow, who I could now see was quite busy fending off both a giant spider and a dark, heavily wrinkled figure with oversized lips that looked very much like my Great Aunt Martha, called out to me once more.

"No, this is no good!" he shouted. "There are too many of them! If you chase every one of these, you'll never get to the monster behind it all!"

"Well then, what do I do?" I asked.

"Ignore these," Bigelow instructed. "Concentrate on finding the hidden beast!"

"How do I do that?" I shouted.

"Focus!" he yelled. "Something happened a few weeks ago. Something that set the beast free. What was it?"

I shuddered.

"I...I don't...remember..."

"Don't hide from it, Will!" Bigelow said. "Face it! Use the light!"

"N..No! I don't want to..."

But just then I heard voices. They emerged from the din and closed in around me, as though a crowd of people was approaching from all directions. Through the misty shadows, one voice came through much clearer, and closer than the others.

"Hey, pipsqueak!" It called to me with deep echoes floating all around. "What are you doing here?"

"He's here, Will!" Bigelow shouted. "Use the light!"

I slowly pointed the light in the direction of the voice. I expected some slimy creature with gruesome tentacles, hideous fangs, and flame for eyes, but it was something much worse. I started shaking when the light revealed...

"It...It's just a *kid*!" Bigelow said.

"A really *big* kid," I said bitingly. Bigelow nodded knowingly.

"A bully," he said.

I nodded.

"But how do I make him go away?"

"Face him!" Bigelow yelled.

"But the light isn't working! He's not shrinking!"

"He is!" Bigelow insisted. "You just can't see it!"

"No! He's getting bigger!" I yelled.

"Face him!" Bigelow commanded.

"But I'm not big enough!" I cried.

"You are!" Bigelow called out. "You're big where it counts most! You trusted me, even though you knew I was a monster. You gave me Teddy when I needed him, even though *you* were afraid too. You *are* big, Will. You're much bigger than him. Everything else is an illusion!"

I pointed the light at the bully. He didn't shrink.

"You can do it, Will!" Bigelow said.

I bit my trembling lip, and then shined the flashlight right on the monster's face.

"I'm not scared of you," I said. He just smiled.

"Yes you are," he said, and grew some more.

He was right.

"What do I do now, Bigelow?" I pleaded.

"Use the light," he said. *"Trust* the light. Look closer."

I don't know how I did it, but I stepped closer to the monster. My hands shook as I held the light up close to his face. Somehow, with the light shining on him, I saw something *behind* the monstrous smile. There was flicker of doubt, a twinge of...

"I *am* scared of you," I admitted. "But you...I see it now...*you're scared too!*"

As quickly as the words sprung from my mouth, his smile vanished. Tears began streaming down his face. I blinked, and saw that Bigelow was right: it *had* been shrinking, I just couldn't see it before.

"Why?" I said to the monster. "Why are *you* scared?"

The monster didn't speak. There, in the glare of the light, he became a boy no bigger than me, cowering in a darkened room, alone but for the tiny flopping guppy that had fallen there earlier. Beside him lay a leather belt, and there were welts showing through the back of his shirt. I actually felt sorry for him. Just then, Bigelow stepped beside me.

"I'm afraid," he said, "That this one is going to hang around for quite a long time."

"That's okay," I said. "If I don't go in the water, the shark can't hurt me."

Bigelow rolled his eyes again.

"I meant the *bully*," he said.

I looked down at Bigelow and smiled.

"So did I," I said. Bigelow smiled back at me. I turned back to the bully, but he was already gone.

"Hiding," Bigelow said. "That means the beast's last defense has fallen."

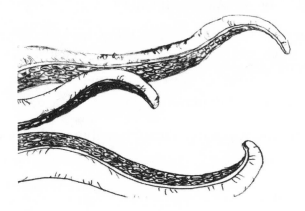

Chapter Eight – The Hidden Beast

I dropped my smile. It fell on the floor and scurried into the closet like a frightened hamster.

"What are you saying?" I sputtered. "Wasn't *that* the beast?"

"No," Bigelow said. "But he was the one who set the beast free."

"Then...then where *is* the..."

"Hush!" Bigelow cut me off, putting a hairy finger to his oversized lips. "*Listen.*"

I pricked up my ears, and heard another voice emerge slowly, softly from the darkness. Though it was very faint at first, I recognized the voice instantly.

"Will," the voice called out.

I knew right then who it was, knew he was the beast.

"Will...it's me..."

"No..." I whimpered. "Oh, no...please..."

But from the black fog ahead, horrible tentacles shot out at me. I stepped back, and stumbled to the ground. I jumped right up and desperately staggered back, trying to escape.

"Will, I..."

"*No!*" I cried. "Leave me alone!"

But the monster did not leave me alone. Instead, flames suddenly burst from the darkness, driving me into a corner just as hideous claws leapt from the shadows and tried to rake at me.

"Use the Revealer, Will!" Bigelow called out. "Point the light at the monster and face the truth about your fear!"

"No!" I shouted. "I don't want to! Just make it go away!"

But the monster kept advancing.

"Will," the monster's voice echoed. "I...don't..."

"*Nooooo!*" I pleaded, tears streaming down my face.

"I...don't...love you."

Backed into a corner with no hope of escape, I finally lifted my flashlight and shined its beam at the monster. There, in the glow of the light, the tentacles and claws vanished, and standing before me, steady and unflinching, was the hidden beast.

My father.

"Nooooo!" I moaned. I dropped the flashlight, and

fell sobbing to the floor. "No, it's not true!"

"It's *not* true," Bigelow's steady voice called out. He shined his flashlight on the beast, who squinted, but held his ground.

"I don't love you, Will," the beast said, growing larger with each echo of my sobs.

"It's not true, Will!" Bigelow shouted. I lifted my head.

"It *is* true," I bawled. "I told my dad about the bully. I told him that I told a teacher, but the teacher didn't do anything! I told him it just wasn't fair! Do you know what he said to me? He said, *'The world's not fair Will. Get used to it.'* Can you believe that?"

"Use your Revealer, Will!" Bigelow shouted, "See the *whole* truth! The light from *my* Revealer alone is not strong enough for this! We have to do it together!"

I stopped sobbing, and looked up at the beast, who was now as big as a house. He looked so smug, it got me angry.

"Come on, Will! I know you have it in you!" Bigelow said.

I stared at the face of the beast, who looked down at me with the contempt my father had in his eyes the day he found out I'd quit pee-wee football. It was the scariest thing I'd ever seen.

"Think you're pretty tough, don't you?" I said to it. "You think you're so much stronger than I am! Well, surprise! I'm a lot stronger than you think! So take this!"

I picked up my flashlight and shined it in his face. Together with Bigelow's light, it made him cower.

"That's it!" Bigelow exclaimed. "That's it! Look at him! See the truth!"

And as I watched, the beast shuddered, and shook its head violently, as though a bee had flown up its nose. Its temple began to swell, and the beast smacked it repeatedly until finally a *telephone* grew out of its ear. I don't think it liked having a phone stuck to its ear, because it scratched and clawed at it, but couldn't make it go away. Then a voice came out of the phone.

"I'm sorry, Mr. Allen," it said in a voice that sounded suspiciously like my principal, Ms. Greevey.

"Not sorry enough!" my father's voice shouted back. It was kind of funny, because the beast covered its mouth to try and keep the words from coming out, but I heard them loud and clear just the same.

"Not *nearly* as sorry as you *will* be," my father's voice continued, as the beast scratched and pulled at its own mouth, to no avail. "Not as sorry as you'll be if this ever happens again!"

"My dad did that?" I turned to Bigelow. "Why didn't he tell me?"

"Look some more," Bigelow urged. I turned back.

A chair had grown out of the beast's behind, growing larger as he shrank, until his feet were pushed out from under him, and he was forced to sit. He looked like a three year old on a throne, struggling mightily to free himself, but then another voice spoke up, and he grabbed at his mouth again. It was my mother's voice.

"Will it help?" she asked.

"I don't know," my father's voice answered. The beast pulled at its mouth and stretched it several feet off its face, but my father's voice still came out clearly.

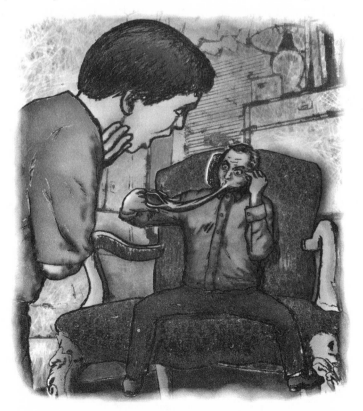

"I don't know," he said despairingly. "They can't watch every bully every moment of the day in every inch of the school. But what else can we do?"

I just stared.

"Daddy?" I said timidly as I stepped toward him. "Daddy...You...*You're* scared too?"

The phone and the chair melted. The beast tried to put its mouth back into place, but it was hopelessly stretched. I stepped right up to it and shined the light on its face. It shrunk down to...well, *daddy* size. Just the right size to do what needed to be done. Somehow, I just knew exactly what that was.

"That's it," Bigelow urged. "Go on..."

I stepped forward and gave the beast a great big hug.

"Nooooo!" it cried out, and began shaking all over. I let go of the beast and stepped back. It shook, and rattled, and finally split open. Light poured out of the cracks while the beast tried desperately to hold itself together, but then finally, there was a gigantic explosion, filling the room like the sun, wiping away the beast and all of the remaining monsters in one great burst of light. When the glow faded, all that remained was Bigelow, me, and some weird new happy meal sized toys together in a darkened room.

"That was him?" I concluded. "That was my big,

horrible monster?"

"Yes," Bigelow said.

I looked at him.

"What a wimp," I snickered. Bigelow chuckled.

"So," I asked. "Is it over now?"

"Almost. You still have one more monster to face."

Chapter Nine – The Final Monster

"Bigelow, do you mean...*you*?" I asked. "I have to face *you*?"

"Yes. You recognize me now, don't you, Will?"

"N...No, I don't."

"You do." Bigelow insisted.

I looked down.

"But I don't want *you* to go away," I said quietly.

"I won't," he assured me. "I promise."

Just then, I looked down at Teddy and realized I had been squeezing him tightly in one arm all this time.

"It looks like he's been squeezed like that a lot,"

Bigelow observed.

"Yes," I told him. "He always made me feel safe when I was scared. I used to take him everywhere. But then…"

I trailed off. I remembered what had happened, and I started getting very upset.

"I…I lost him. We were on vacation, and I lost him. I was afraid I would never see him again."

As I said this, Bigelow grew. In just a few seconds, the trench coat wasn't dragging on the floor anymore, and long, hairy arms were coming out of the sleeves.

"But then we found him!" I cried out. "We found him! I hugged him so hard. I wouldn't let go of him the whole trip home, and then I brought him back up to my room. I've never taken him out of my room since."

I looked at Bigelow.

"You're still growing," I said.

"Yes," Bigelow answered.

I looked down at Teddy, and gave him a great, big hug.

"I love you, Teddy," I told him as I squeezed him hard. Then I turned to Bigelow. He was huge now, standing almost from floor to ceiling, with great hairy legs showing beneath his coat.

"Here," I said, as I put Teddy in those great, hairy arms. "He's yours now. Take good care of him."

And that's when the most amazing thing happened. Bigelow looked at me and smiled, with giant, razor sharp teeth shining out from his crescent shaped, ear-to-ear mouth. And he started to glow. He glowed brighter and brighter, and as he shone, he shrank. By the time the glow faded, he was back to his original size.

"You're looking better," I told him. He smiled.

"So are you," he said.

I smiled too. It was probably the biggest smile I ever smiled.

"You'll be okay now," he said. "No monsters will bother you anymore."

"All thanks to you," I said gratefully. "You really are a great monster detective."

"So are you," he said. "You know, the monster detective business is very short-handed at the moment. Maybe you could help out."

"But...I'm not a monster," I reminded him.

"Oh, that's not what your mother says," Bigelow answered. Then he made a big smile to show me he was joking.

I think.

"Anyway, you're smart, and brave, and you know what to do now. That should be enough."

"But how will people find me? *You* at least have a business card."

"Now you do too," he said. "Just look."

I reached into my pocket and took out Bigelow's card.
It now read:

I looked back at Bigelow, who still wore that great big
smile. He handed me a magnifying glass and a silver
badge.

I lifted the glass and used it to look all over my room.
When I turned to my shelf, the tiny toilet monster sitting
there glowed eerily through the lens.

"Wow!" I said, "My very own monster spyglass!"

"Monsterscope," Bigelow corrected. "It's called a
Monsterscope. That, the Revealer, and your own wits and
bravery are the only tools you need to do the job."

"Well, thanks," I said, lowering the glass. "I just
hope I don't have to get paid in teddy bears."

"That reminds me," Bigelow said. "Look."

He pointed at my bed. There, sitting next to the pillow,

was Teddy. This time I was *sure* that he was smiling too.

"How did he get...But...but Bigelow, he's yours now," I protested. "You earned him fair and square."

"Yes I did," he agreed. "We should always earn our friends. And keep earning them. Remember I promised you that I would give him a home where he would always be happy?"

I nodded.

"Well, I can think of no place in the world where my friend Teddy would be happier than right there on your bed. Just as long as he gets to come with me on an adventure now and then."

I rushed up and gave Bigelow a big hug. He seemed to like it, even if it did make him shrink some more.

"MMMERRFF...Easy...does...it..." he managed to get out in a muffled voice. I let him go and stepped back.

"Sorry," I said. "It looks like I made you even smaller."

"Just remember," Bigelow said, "Size isn't everything. A little person..."

"Can solve some really big cases," I finished. He just smiled again.

"And you are very big where it counts most," he told me, and turned to my bed. He leaned over and stuck his head underneath, but then looked back, gave me a playful wink, and climbed on top and crawled under the covers. There, beside his new friend Teddy, he formed a great lump that gradually shrank, until the blanket lay flat on the bed. Teddy smiled happily, feeling his friend, though unseen, still there beside him.

"Everything else is just an illusion," I recalled. Then I put out the light and climbed into bed.

Chapter 10 - Beginnings

The next morning, I got out of bed, gave Teddy a hug, and went and checked the shelf. There, sitting among my books, camera, and baseball glove were a plastic guppy, a two-inch tall tree that cowered shyly, and a tiny toy toilet with the personality of a snapping turtle.

"Good morning, fellas," I said. "How are you doing

today?"

None of them seemed at all pleased. Maybe one day, they would get tired of hanging around, but until then, I thought I might get a terrarium for them or something. If I figured out what to feed them, they would make very interesting pets.

On the way out of the kitchen after breakfast I surprised my mom and dad by giving them each a big hug. Once they got over the shock they seemed to like it, even though it made my dad gag on his scrambled eggs a little. Or maybe that was because there was something hard and chunky in them again. With my mom's cooking, you can never be sure. Anyway, I met up with Jeannine on the ride to school and told her all about what happened the night before. She seemed a little skeptical, until I showed her my new business card and silver badge.

"Monster detective!" she exclaimed. "You, Will, a monster detective! Oh, I'm so jealous!"

"Don't be," I said. "You can be my partner."

Jeannine turned red. Her mother was right: it's not her color.

"Oh, Will! Do you mean it?" she practically gushed. "Me, your partner?"

"Sure," I said. "Sherlock Holmes has Dr. Watson, doesn't he? All detectives have partners. Or secretaries, at least."

"Oh, this will be so great!" she said. "You can do the snooping, and the fighting monsters stuff, and I can..."

Her smile faded a bit.

"Um, what exactly can I do?"

"Well, you can do the case logs," I suggested. "And the research. You're aces at that. There's lots of stuff to look up when you run a detective business, I'll bet. And you can handle publicity. You're much better at talking to people than I am."

Jeannine smiled at that, but then it faded again.

"You know Will," she said. "Now that I think about it, how are we going to find any clients? Are we going to advertise or something?"

I thought about that.

"Hmmm," I said. "I don't think so. If word gets around, we'll have a lot of people making fun of us all the time. Who wants that?"

Jeannine started scratching her head.

"Well, what do we do?" she said.

Just then, a boy we didn't know walked up to us. Jeannine and I both quickly froze. At first his eyes darted

about nervously, but then he looked right at me.

"Will Allen?" he said.

I looked at him. He was a whole lot taller than either me or Jeannine, with long red hair and very big glasses.

"Yes, that's me," I answered suspiciously.

"Are you Will Allen, the monster detective?" he asked.

Jeannine and I turned to each other. She looked just as shocked as I did.

"Who wants to know?" I asked.

"My name's Timmy. Timmy Newsome. I need your help."

He looked around, and then leaned in very close and whispered, "I have a monster in my closet."

I looked at Jeannine, and then back at Timmy and asked, "How did you find me?"

"I don't know how," he said. "But your business card was in my backpack this morning."

He handed it to me, and when I saw what was on it, my mouth fell open, which was sort of a bad thing to have happen, since my gum fell out onto the floor of the bus. I passed the card over to Jeannine, whose eyes grew wide as she read:

Jeannine and I just looked at each other and smiled.

"So," I said to Timmy. "What's eating you?"

That's a little monster detective joke.

Okay, a *very* little monster detective joke.

But then, it's not so bad to be very little, is it? After all, a little person can solve some really big cases.

So that's how it all began. But if you think things got easy after that, think again. In fact, before I even began investigating my first case, I discovered that being a detective was going to be a lot tougher than I thought.

But that's another story.

The adventure continues in

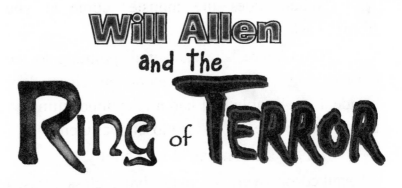

Will Allen
and the
Ring of Terror

Will discovers that being a monster detective requires much more than just brains and bravery.

But when his very first client, Timmy Newsome, is tormented by strange images that Will does not understand, can even Jeannine's timely assistance help him solve the mystery and reveal Timmy's true monster in time to save them all from the razor-sharp claws of a terrifying **HARPY**?

…I pulled out my flashlight and magnifying glass, the special ones that Bigelow had given me, then I went to the light switch and turned it off.

The room went dark, but some hazy moonlight filtered through the mist surrounding the windows and gave everything within an eerie blue glow.

"Where does the monster come at you from?" I asked.

"Over there," he answered, pointing to the corner of his room. There stood the closet door beside a small table that had a telephone sitting on top. "They come out of the closet over there."

"I'll go check it out," I said boldly.

I walked on over, my magnifying glass pressed to my face, searching for signs of monsters. Inch by inch I crept, flashlight at the ready, to the closet door. There was no sign of anything strange in the sight of my magnifying glass, but the air became stale with the odor of rotting fish, growing more and more foul with every step I took. That made me edgy.

"I...I'm going in," I announced, and gently prodded the door.

Before I could even gasp, it flew open with a loud, creaking howl, and something dark and slimy fell upon me.

"OH...OH MY GOD!" I shouted.

"IT'S SO HORRIBLE..."

Jason Edwards is a schoolteacher, husband, and a father of two young daughters. This book was originally written for his elder daughter to help her deal with some painful anxieties. It is his hope that as Will Allen changes from a boy who is crushed by his fears to one who masters them, so too will young readers everywhere.

Jason lives in New York with his wife and children. He loves reading and telling stories to children at schools and libraries. He also loves receiving letters from his readers, and can be contacted at:

Jason@RogueBearPress.com

Kids!

Are <u>you</u> brave enough to face your fears?

Then you too can become an associate member of the Monster Detective Agency! It's **FREE !!**

Just write your name and E-mail address on a piece of paper and send it to:

Monster Detective Agency
c/o Rogue Bear Press
P.O. Box #513
Ardsley, NY. 10502

Or fill out the application on our website, **MonsterDetectiveAgency.com.**

You will receive:

- o Your very own MDA business card!
- o Special Monster Detective mysteries and puzzles!
- o A Monster Detective E-newsletter with club-only profiles and illustrations of your favorite Monster Detective characters, plus details of upcoming Monster Detective events!
- o Club-only merchandise offers, including Monster Detective T-shirts, pens, and spyglasses!